MARVEL
SPIDER-MAN
Homecoming

BOOK OF THE FILM

EGMONT

We bring stories to life

First published in Great Britain 2017 by Egmont UK Limited
The Yellow Building, 1 Nicholas Road, London W11 4AN

Adapted by Jim McCann

Directed by Jon Watts
Produced by Kevin Feige and Amy Pascal
Based on the screenplay by
Jonathan Goldstein & John Francis Daley and
Jon Watts & Christopher Ford and
Chris McKenna & Erik Sommers

ISBN 978 1 4052 8830 9

67838/1

Printed and bound by CPI Group (UK) Ltd, Croydon, CR0 4YY

PROLOGUE

The famous skyline of New York City shimmered in the morning light as the sun danced across Avengers Tower. Home to the greatest Super Heroes on Earth. Yes, the world had Super Heroes now. Billionaire geniuses in iron suits. World War II super soldiers. Even godlike beings from other worlds wielding mystical hammers. New Yorkers thought they had seen everything until one fateful day when the sky opened up and a full-scale alien invasion rained from a portal above. Monstrous beings known as the Chitauri crashed into buildings and wreaked havoc in the streets. Fortunately for Earth, the Avengers assembled and drove them back, saving the day and announcing their presence on a global scale. After that, it was time for New Yorkers to do what they did best: move on with life.

And clean up. There was always the cleanup...

Deep inside a roped-off tunnel of Grand Central Terminal, music blared from a radio as a salvage crew hacked, hammered, and torched its way to try to break through the hide of one of the Chitauri serpents. The crew's boss, Adrian Toomes, smiled as he paused and addressed his workers.

"Now, see, fellas, you can't just saw your way through this stuff like normal. These beasties are crafty," he said, a glint in his eye as he raised his hammer. He swung it down on a piece of alien tech embedded in the serpent's hide, and the tech flew off, landing in his hand. "Gotta use their own tech against them."

Toomes was tossing the Chitauri tech onto the back of his truck when he spied a member of his crew trying to sneak by.

"Afternoon, Brice!" he called out. "So glad you could make it."

Brice stopped, busted. "Sorry, boss," he replied. "Alarm didn't go off."

Toomes looked over at another member of his crew, who was tinkering with a generator. "Hey, Mason, think you can whip up Brice an alarm that only plays this one song?" he said, reaching for his phone. "Here, let me cue it up."

"Please, Toomes," Brice pleaded, knowing what song it was. "Anything but that."

"Gotta pay the piper, Bri—" Toomes started

to respond, before being cut off by the sudden appearance of men and women in crisp suits and shiny hard hats. The badges on their uniforms identified them as some sort of governmental agency, but Toomes didn't recognize it. A stern-looking woman, obviously in charge, stepped forward, with another agent at her left flank. Toomes turned off the music, ready for a standoff.

"Attention, please," the woman announced. "In accordance with Executive Order 396-B, all post-battle cleanup operations are now under our jurisdiction! Thank you for your service. We'll take it from here now."

"Who are you?" Toomes demanded.

"Qualified personnel," answered the man at her side, pointing at his badge.

"Qualified? I'm not the one with the price tag still on my hard hat, Agent...Foster, is it?"

Toomes sneered and laughed. His crew chuckled behind him.

The woman remained firm. "You can collect your tools and go," she said as she and Foster turned to leave. Toomes circled around her, noting the name on her badge.

"Look, Agent Hoag—"

"*Director* Hoag," she corrected him.

"Director. You can't do this. I got a contract with the city," Toomes insisted.

Her face was unmoved as she responded, "All salvage contracts are now void."

"I bought trucks for this job, put on more guys!" Toomes snapped, his voice beginning to rise. "They've got families! So do I!"

Hoag met his pleas with silence. Toomes's face flushed with anger.

"Okay, okay, I'm a smart man," he said, taking

a breath and leaning in to whisper. "I've been trying to do this the right way, but if there's someone
I have to pay...y'know..."

Hoag looked at him with disdain. "The only
thing you have to do is turn over any exotic materials in your possession and leave."

"C'mon, lady," he practically begged, "I'm all
in on this thing. You pull the plug, I'm gonna lose
my house."

"I don't know what to tell you, sir," Hoag replied
coolly.

Foster had a smug look on his face now. "Maybe
next time, don't overextend yourself," he said.

That was all Toomes could handle. Without
thinking, he swung at Agent Foster with a hard
right hook, connecting across the man's jaw. Foster and the other agents immediately drew their
guns. Toomes's crew picked up their tools. The
air was tense, both sides ready for a fight.

Finally, Hoag motioned for her men to lower their weapons.

"Mr. Toomes, we are done here," she said, her voice quiet, but steady. "You have your instructions. If you have a grievance, you'll have to take it up with my superiors." She walked off as the other agents began to call in orders for their cleanup crews to take over the site.

Toomes was left speechless, along with the rest of his crew members, who started making their way to their trucks. Finally, he called out after her: "*Who* are your superiors?"

On a beat-up television screen, a TV news reporter stood outside Grand Central Terminal as agents dressed just like the ones that Toomes had encountered moved intently through a cordoned-off section. In the background, Agent Foster was directing a group of men in brand-new workmen's uniforms and the same shiny hard hats he wore.

"Announced today," the reporter said, "a joint venture between Stark Industries and the federal government, the newly created Department of Damage Control will oversee collection and storage of alien and other exotic materials—"

"Shut it off!" Toomes bellowed.

He and his crew were in the workshop of Toomes Salvage Company, still sulking about the day's blow to the business. The workshop was a large building that held a fleet of trucks and equipment. Toomes wasn't lying when he said he'd invested his life's savings in the Battle of New York cleanup contract.

He hurled a bottle, narrowly missing the television. "So now the jerks like Stark who made this mess get paid to clean it up?" he grumbled.

"And we're out of a job," said Mason, absent-mindedly tinkering with his tools.

Another of Toomes's crew, Schultz, raised his glass in a toast. "Here's to the little guys like us! Work hard, pay your dues, and always get it in the end!"

The rest of the crew gave halfhearted cheers and raised their glasses, but Toomes was in too foul a mood. His eyes were on one of the trucks. Nearby, Brice followed Toomes's gaze and saw something peeking out from under the tarp that covered the back of the truck. His eyes widened, and he moved in for a closer look.

"Is this what I think it is?" Brice asked as Mason came over to join him.

"Some of that alien tech from the site," Mason said. His mind racing, he turned to Toomes and asked, "Should we turn it over?"

Toomes didn't respond immediately. His eyes were fixed on a child's drawing on his desk. A simple stick-figure drawing of a dad, a mom, and a little girl in front of a house. It seemed out of place in the grimy workroom. But it was clearly special to Toomes; he kept it in a place where he would always see it, a beacon of hope among the rubble. Finally turning his attention away from the drawing, he looked over at Brice and Mason.

"No," he answered, his voice low. "Bring it into your workshop, Mason."

Brice and Mason exchanged an uneasy glance, but one look at Toomes's darkened face told them it was best not to question their boss's orders. As Toomes watched the men unload the tech from the truck, the gears in his mind began to turn. After all, he was—just as he told Hoag—a very smart man...

CHAPTER 1

"**N**ew York. Queens." A booming voice set the stage as buildings whizzed past the lens of a camera. "It's a rough borough. But hey, it's home. Hard to say good-bye, but the world's not gonna save itself. Sometimes a hero—"

A slightly annoyed voice chimed in. "Who are you talking to?"

"Huh? Oh, no one..." The booming voice

cracked a little. "No one. I'm just making a video of the trip."

Okay, okay, it was actually *my* voice. And maybe it wasn't so booming.

I held up my phone to the driver of the limo to show him. This entire day had been unreal. Can you imagine me, Peter Parker, of all people, in the back of a limo? And not just any limo—a limo owned by Tony Stark and driven by his bodyguard, Happy Hogan! (I still don't know how he ended up with that nickname—"Happy" hadn't smiled once since picking me up.)

"You know you can't show that to anybody, right?" he grumbled.

"Yeah, I know." Who would I even show it to anyway?

"Then why were you using that voice?" Happy continued.

"Just for…fun. Y'know…" I tried to lighten

the mood by giving a smile, but I think it looked more like my just showing the dentist my teeth.

"Uh-huh," Happy grunted.

Before I could stop them, the words flew out of my mouth: "So why do they call you 'Happy'?"

The partition raised slowly in response, ending the discussion.

"Cool, I get it, not much of a talker." Happy didn't seem nearly as excited as I was to be taking this trip. But at least with the partition closed, I could go back to my filming in private. "Where was I? Oh yeah. Sometimes a hero has to fly off when duty calls..."

If Tony Stark's limo was cool, his jet (at his own private airport, naturally) was *insanely cool*! The seats swiveled and were made with real leather; TVs were everywhere, along with a working Avengers pinball machine!

I accepted the cream soda one of the flight attendants offered me and turned to Happy. "Uh, is there a bathroom, or should I ... ?" I asked preemptively.

"First time on a private plane?" Happy said with ... was that a smile? Or a smirk?

Blushing, I admitted, "First time on any plane."

After recording the full tour of the plane (which did, indeed, have a bathroom), it was time to take off. The jet roared, and soon we were over the Atlantic. Happy snored the entire way, giving my video journal a gravelly soundtrack, but the scenery made up for it. Before I knew it, we were flying over Western Europe and descending into Germany.

Everything after that seemed like a blur. Another limo. Speeding past really old architecture. Being ushered into a hotel room that was almost the size of May's apartment in Queens and a hundred times nicer (not that I'd ever tell her that). The phone call saying, "Mr. Stark will be arriving in ten minutes." Ten minutes—*ten minutes!* I wasn't even dressed yet!

The knock on the door came just as I pulled my mask over my head. "Come—ahem—" *Sound more confident, Parker,* I scolded myself. "Come in."

But he was already in. And it wasn't Tony Stark. It was Happy. He walked right in without a word and stared at me. What was he staring at? Then he waved his hand at me, his face looking confused, with a hint of impatience.

"What *is* this?" was all he said, still staring.

"My…suit…?" I took a guess that he wasn't talking about the room's décor.

He looked confused, glancing around the room. "Didn't you get a box? There was supposed to be a box," he muttered, mostly to himself. He walked through a small doorway into an adjoining room and spotted it. "There's a box."

I walked in to see him pointing to a dresser. I hadn't even bothered to explore the multiple rooms of my hotel room. It was a box, all right. And it came with a note: *A minor upgrade.—TS.* I pressed a button, and the case opened.

So far, I'd been excited by the limo, blown away by the jet, and astounded by the hotel. But this… this was…

"Whoa." I couldn't muster any other words. It was an amazing, beautiful, shiny, magnificent work of art. It made my hand-sewn Spidey outfit look like a cheap Halloween costume. This—this was a Spider-Man *uniform*! I was still trying to absorb everything in front of me when the open case unfolded even more, revealing compartments filled with accessories, like web cartridges and some other things that I really hoped came with a user's manual.

"This is *way* better than mine!" I blurted out.

"Now," Happy said, folding his arms as a serious look crossed his face, "ready to earn it?"

Oh man. I should have asked what he meant by "earn it." I went to an airstrip with the Avengers to fight...other Avengers? Oh well. Gotta trust the boss man. But this was definitely going in my video journal. I webbed my phone to the wing of an airplane, hit RECORD, and...

"Whoa, there's Iron Man—and the War Machine guy—and the Romanoff lady." No need to use a booming voice to narrate the video; I was too excited to keep my cool. "Black Panther is *awesome*!"

"Underoos!" Iron Man yelled as he and the others prepared for the showdown.

"That's my cue," I said, looking into the camera. "I gotta *steal* Captain America's shield! Wish me luck!"

THWIP! I shot some web, grabbing Cap's shield and yanking it as I flipped onto a truck. Man, that felt . . . freaking, terrifyingly great!

"Hey, everybody!" I said as I landed.

Then the action really started.

Thank goodness I got it all on video, because I can hardly remember most of it. I remember fighting against Captain America and his physics-defying shield, and seeing everyone's powers and skills. I remember trying to figure out if the purple guy flying straight at me was on our side or not. I remember taking down the giant-size Ant-Man old-school *Empire Strikes Back*—style. Yup, it's moments like those that phone cameras were made for . . .

"I thought I was gonna freeze up after Tony yelled out 'Underoos.'" I was back in my hotel room, watching and rewatching the video over and over, doing my own postgame breakdown. "Then I grabbed Cap's shield like—*PFSHEWWWWW!*"

I was so into reliving the moment that I didn't notice I'd flicked my wrist and fired a web. Only this time it didn't shoot out like my regular webbing; it was more like a ball that bounced all over the room, zooming over my head, almost hitting a lamp, making way too much noise as it hit the walls and ceiling and floor. Finally, it landed—*SPLAT*—in a gooey pile of webbing right by the hotel doorway.

Unfortunately, standing *in* the doorway, his face inches away from a mouthful of webbing, was Happy. In his pajamas. Heh, Happy wore pajamas. As usual, he wasn't smiling.

"This hotel has thin walls—" he started.

"Right," I said, trying not to let my excitement show too much, "you are absolutely right; won't happen again. Sorry, Happy!"

Happy gave me a look that suggested he wanted to continue his scolding, but sleep won out in the end. "Go to bed," he said, shutting the door. "We leave first thing."

As soon as he was gone, I examined the web cartridge on my wrist. A holographic display read RICOCHET WEB. *"Cooooool,"* I whispered.

Everything was so freaking cool. I heard Happy's voice in my head telling me to go to sleep. I tugged at my glove to start changing out of my suit when another voice popped into my head. My voice. *I wonder what else this suit can do.* My head-voice drowned out Happy's as I grabbed my phone, webbed it to my chest, and started to climb out the window.

20

Out of the corner of my eye, I saw myself in the mirror.

"Shhhhhhh," I told my mirror-self as I swung out into the German night.

I burrowed my face into my pillow and snuggled in deeper. Beds in Germany felt so much better than the ones in Queens.

Queens!

I opened my eyes and sat up so fast I almost flipped out of bed. Happy's words echoed in my head. *We leave first thing.* First thing? What time was first thing? Clocks didn't have "first thing" on them, but it was probably second or third past first thing. I glanced in the mirror and realized my suit was still on. I must have fallen asleep after saving that old lady from being mugged last night.

How long was I out? No time to think about

it. I had to get out of this awesome suit, pack my stuff, and hit up the breakfast bar before Happy came to get me. No way could I fly back to New York with an empty stomach *plus* a grumpy Happy.

The plan was going all right so far. I was inches away from the fluffiest Belgian waffle I'd ever seen when a familiar shadow seemed to cover the entire breakfast bar. Without a word, Happy nodded for me to follow him as he turned and walked to his table. Looking back at the glorious waffle, I made a silent promise: *One day...*

I flopped into the seat opposite Happy, and we had a ten-second stare-off. Ten. Long. Seconds. Finally, he cut into a waffle (no fair!) and didn't even look at me before his interrogation began.

"Late night Spider-Man-ing," he said. It wasn't

a question. Somehow he knew. Of course he knew.

I stared at the waffle longingly before I realized he was waiting for an answer.

"It was nighttime, and just a few people saw me," I explained. "They cheered and waved. No one here knows Spider-Man. And, anyway, I look *wayyyyyy* different now." I was talking faster than I could think. "Oh, and some club kids might start dressing up as me, but that's it, I promise!"

Happy lifted a newspaper off the table. "Just a few people?"

The headline was in German so I had no idea what it meant. *"Der Klebrige Junge Rettet Bundeskanzler!"* I read aloud, trying not to butcher each word too much. "Huh?"

"Sticky Boy Saves Chancellor," Happy translated.

"Ohhhhhh! That old lady was the chancellor?

No wonder she tried to give me such a big tip," I joked, trying to lighten the mood. "Well, at least no one got a photo, right?"

Happy unfolded the paper. The bottom half had a splash image of me swinging on a web line, the chancellor tucked under my arm. My empty stomach dropped.

"Soooo," I said sheepishly, "I guess I'm probably grounded from the breakfast bar, huh?"

Happy wiped his mouth with his napkin, stood, grabbed his suitcase, and headed for the exit. I took that as a "yes."

The jet ride back to the States wasn't as fun. Thankfully, Stark had some food on the plane, if you can even call fish eggs and crackers food. I downed some juice and actually managed to sleep a little on the flight. My all-nighter finally caught up to me, I guess.

Even the limo ride back to May's apartment in Queens wasn't as fun. Happy kept the privacy screen up the entire time. This time Tony Stark was actually sitting in the back with me, but he was on his phone most of the time. I was afraid I'd blown everything by making front-page news. Finally, we pulled up a safe distance from the apartment, so we didn't attract too much attention.

We sat in some seriously awkward silence for a moment before Mr. Stark finally said something.

"Ya did good, kid," he said.

I did good? *I did good!*

"Does this mean I'm an Avenger now?" I asked, probably a little too eagerly.

"It definitely does not."

"Oh," I said, trying not to look too crushed as I opened the door.

"Don't forget the box," Stark called out as I turned to leave.

The box! The suit! That meant… "I didn't blow it with the whole chancellor thing? I can keep it?"

"It's yours," Stark replied. "You earned it."

My heart was going a mile a minute. "Awesome!" was all I could reply. Then it hit me. The suit was mine to keep. Iron Man himself was giving me a new uniform.

I was going to be an Avenger.

"So when's our next mission?" I asked, all smiles, as if that was something I asked every day.

"We'll call ya," Stark said, signaling it was time for me to get moving.

"Guess I'll be seeing you around, Happy," I called out as I stood on the sidewalk. The driver window lowered slightly, but there was no answer.

No matter. I waited until the limo had rounded the corner before taking out my phone, turning on the camera, looking right into the lens, and adding one final, important update:

"They're gonna call me!"

CHAPTER 2

"Four months, five days, and eightee—nineteen minutes," I muttered, flinching as someone on the train sneezed right behind my back. "No calls yet..."

The weather had just turned crisp, and everyone in the jam-packed train looked either sick, tired, or sick *and* tired. I had managed to avoid catching a cold since getting my spider-powers, but I sort of knew how they felt.

I looked at the cracked screen on my phone and went back to a happier time, in Germany, when I was totally an Avenger...for, like, ten minutes.

Suddenly, my screen lit up with an incoming call. BLOCKED ID flashed as it rang. It was them! They were calling! I fumbled to answer.

"Parker here! Go for Peter! Parker!" I waited for an ultra-top-secret assignment to come from Mr. Stark. Instead, my shoulders drooped. "No, there's no Lulu here...Ma'am, I can't book your coloring because this isn't a hair salon. Really sorry, though."

I hung up with a heavy sigh, knowing that somewhere a woman with her roots coming through couldn't find Lulu, and I still wasn't an Avenger. Thankfully, we were approaching my train stop.

Taking up almost an entire city block, Midtown School of Science & Technology loomed large as I walked up the sidewalk. It was probably the only place in the city where I fit in. You had your over-achievers, genius-level-yet-stressed-out-obsessive-compulsives, inventors of the next Big Thing, all with at least one overflowing backpack, all filing in to forge new ground and show the world that nerds really would inherit the earth.

Just then, a car sped past me and skidded into the parking entrance. The vanity plate on the car read FLASHDRV. Oh right. And Flash was a student here, too. If I were an Avenger, he'd be my ego-driven, obnoxious arch-villain.

Glancing down at my phone one last time, I entered the school building. I was surrounded by students showing off their newest advances in AI technology, "rebels" furiously hacking their way to exposing corruption online, friends discussing string theory and the probabilities of Stephen

Hawking's multiverse. I had to duck to avoid a drone as I stopped at my locker.

"Guess who got the complete solar system— including all of Jupiter's moons?" a voice rang out. I recognized the speaker even before he leaned against the locker next to mine. Ned, my best friend. And a nonbeliever in personal space. "All for hours of interstellar fun!"

I looked at him in disbelief, my mind blown. "No way!" I said. "That thing's gotta have—"

"Three thousand eight hundred and three pieces." Ned beamed back. "And I built a mini-hover stand so it not only floats, but the moons circle in orbit when assembled!"

"Sick!" I had been waiting for months for that building set to come out.

"Right?" Ned replied, practically shaking with excitement. "So? Wanna build it tonight?"

I did. I really did. But there was something else I wanted to do even more. "I can't," I said. "I got the—"

"Stark internship. I know." I could see his bubble bursting. "You've always got the Stark internship."

"Yeah, and pretty soon it's going to lead to a real job with him," I said, trying to convince both him and myself.

Ned's face lit up. "That would be so sweet, working for Iron Man!" he said. "He'd be all, 'Good job on your spreadsheet, Peter. Here, have a gold coin.'" I wasn't sure which was worse: Ned's Iron Man impression or his idea of gainful employment. "I don't really know how jobs work," he confessed.

I laughed along with him. "No, I'm sure that's exactly it."

"Okay, how about this?" Ned compromised. "I'll knock out Saturn, and then swing by your place so we can finish the rings and moons together."

"Yeah, rings and moons…" I repeated, or I think that's what he said. Another voice had caught my attention.

"…I'll check in on the decorations at lunch, but then I have a meeting with the painters. We need to make sure the right shade for the backdrop…" Liz walked by with the rest of the Homecoming committee, and the entire world seemed to melt away around her.

The ringing of the school bell jolted me from my thoughts.

"Saturn, my place, later," I confirmed with Ned as we parted ways and headed off to another day at school.

8:30 AM. Could this day go any slower? We were only halfway through physics class. While most students were taking notes on their fancy tablets about whatever Ms. Warren was teaching, I turned back to my computer screen to watch more videos. The video of the Avengers fighting aliens in the Battle of New York had millions of views, not counting my 314, roughly. It was five years old, but people were still leaving comments.

"Now, how about calculating thrust? Where do we start? Yes, Flash?" Ms. Warren droned on.

"With the binomial," Flash answered confidently.

"Almost," Ms. Warren replied, the word seeming to take Flash down a notch. I chuckled under my breath, moving on to another video.

"Peter, still with us, I assume?" Ms. Warren's voice rang out.

Busted. *Okay, think, Parker, you got this.* I looked at the impossibly long equation on the whiteboard. The answer was...somewhere... and it was...

"Um...thrust?" I repeated, stalling for time. "Yeah. Ah, solve for *x*, *then* determine the binomial." Whew. That was close.

"Right as always," Ms. Warren said, her praise causing Flash to stare daggers at me. Whatever. The bell was going to ring in three...two...

Lunch. Finally. Sitting at the back table away from the popular kids (yes, there are still popular kids, even at a genius school), Ned was telling me some calculus joke when Liz and her best friend, Betty, started to hang Homecoming banners across the room. I wanted to go tell Liz that it was a little crooked on the left, but Betty whipped out a level and fixed it. Thanks a lot, Betty . . .

"And then I died," Ned suddenly said.

"Sorry," I said. Obviously that was not the end of the joke. "It's just . . . did Liz get a new sweater?"

"No, we've seen that one before," Ned replied. "Not with that skirt, though." He cocked his head slightly. "It's working for her."

I stared at her outfit and agreed that it was definitely working for her. Then I caught myself and noted, "We should stop staring before it gets creepy."

SLAM! A stack of books hit the table, followed by a dry voice, calling us out. "Too late."

It was Michelle, the arty kid in a school of science kids. "You two are such losers," she declared.

"Then why are you sitting with us?" Ned asked, annoyed.

"'Cause I don't have any friends." She shrugged. It was true. "Plus, we're having decathlon practice during lunch." Wait—

"What?" I was not prepared for the onslaught of people who suddenly filled the table. Unfortunately, one of them was Flash. But way more fortunately, another was Liz.

"Not so fast," Liz said as I stood up to make room. "I've trapped you in my web." Awkward. "We figured if you're gonna flake on every practice after school, Parker, we'll just have to practice during school."

She was thinking of me. The warm fuzzies started, followed by the guilt, then interrupted by Flash's condescending snort: "I can't believe we're catering to him. We don't need this dork."

Good. There was my opening to break it to them that—

"As team captain, I disagree," Liz cut in. "If we're gonna win nationals, we need every dork at this table."

Oh boy. This was going to make it tougher to rip off the Band-Aid. "About nationals," I started, causing everyone at the table to stare at me. "I can't go."

My words hung in the air for a second before being met with a chorus of protests (and an insult from Flash), but it was Liz's voice that cut through the noise.

"Why?!" She sounded personally betrayed.

Because I'm Spider-Man! I did absolutely *not* say, even though I wanted to.

"I'm just…I'm really busy right now," I

mumbled. My answer was weak. Even I didn't believe it.

"Doing what?" Michelle asked. "You already quit Computer Club and Robotics Lab." She was right. "Not that I'm obsessed with him; I'm just observant," she told the rest of the table quickly.

Liz looked confused. I could tell she was not pleased. At all. "You can't bail on us a week before nationals," she insisted. "You're our anchor on physics."

"You have . . . Flash," I offered.

The sound of his name inflated his ego even more. "Yeah, you do!" he crowed, high-fiving the air. "Neil deGrasse Tyson's got nothing on me!" I had unleashed a decathlon monster. Everyone else seemed to agree.

"Peter, you're our go-to. We're better off with you," said Abraham, another member of the team.

I tried to reassure them, though I was looking mostly at Liz. "Look, they wouldn't do a physics challenge two years in a row," I reasoned. "You guys have this." I turned to the rest of the group. "I'm really sorry. But you're all awesome. Good luck." I grabbed my backpack and started to walk away, but Liz caught my arm before I could leave.

"Peter, look, I get it. It's hard to juggle everything, especially sophomore year," she said, trying to be understanding. "But we were counting on you." I could feel her grip tighten a little.

"I'm sorry," I said, not able to meet her eyes.

"Don't you wanna go to DC?" she pressed. "See the White House? Stay in a fancy hotel?"

"I do. But I...I just can't." I freed my arm from her grip and ran off.

I could faintly hear Liz's voice as she turned to the rest of the team. "What does Peter Parker have to do that's so important?"

It was time for me to make some more web fluid. Also known as chemistry class. While the teacher talked excitedly about the solutions we'd be mixing today, I was at my lab station in the back, working on my own solution.

This was the one class I looked forward to, mainly so I could keep concocting my special formula here and not have May walk in on me refilling these bad boys. I took out a pair of metal cartridges and filled them with my own science project. And just in time, because the bell would be going off any—

RIIIIIIIIIIIING!

Freedom! I was out the door and three blocks away before Flash could even get to his car. I hopped on the train and made it back to Queens, where I made my regular pit stop at Mr. Dalmar's bodega. Five dollars got me my usual—a pack of gummi worms and a number four sandwich, pressed flat with extra pickles.

Next, it was off to my "Stark internship." I hated lying to Ned and my friends, but I justified it by rationalizing that I was kinda-sorta *technically* an Avengers intern. I ducked into an alley and pulled my Spidey suit out of my backpack. Then, it was just one...foot...in front of the— ew, foot in garbage! Foot in garbage!—watching out for the dumpster, definitely didn't need a concussion half dressed like this.

Finally—once my suit was on—came the part I loved the most. I pushed the spider-button on my chest, and the suit practically came to life, whirling and contracting skintight. I tossed my backpack with my regular clothes into the air and— *THWIP!*— webbed it to the dumpster, out of sight. I had to set my watch alarm; I did have a curfew, after all. Then I crawled up the side of the building and looked out over pretty much the entire neighborhood. In Queens, you can do that from about four stories up.

Looking out, I saw the city. My city. Ready to be made better by Spider-Man. I grinned under my mask. "Let's get to work..."

CHAPTER 3

I pictured my eyes narrowing (the lenses built into this suit actually changed shape with my expression!) as I searched for criminals, delinquents, and ne'er-do-wells wherever they lurked. It wasn't long at all before...

Shots fired! Gunshots!

...from a video game. Crisis averted.

A scream from the alley behind me! I flipped backward, ready to take on my foe...A man taking out the trash from the pizzeria, who screamed again.

Rats—literally. Two huge rats stood between him and the dumpster. I sighed. It was going to be a long day.

CLINK! THUNK! Now, those noises I recognized. Looking down the block confirmed it— yup, we had a robbery in progress. Someone had just cut the chain off a bike.

Time to be a hero.

I jumped into action, web-swinging down the block, closing in on the thief. Man, this was the stuff. The kind of action I lived for, that made me count the hours down at school. The stuff that would make me an Avenger (or at least get a callback). Flipping through the air, I landed right in front of the would-be bicycle bandit, stopping him in his tracks.

"That's not your bike," I said in my best Super Hero voice.

"Says who?" the guy challenged.

Huh. They usually ran away at this point. "Says..." I searched my brain for what to say next. Aha! Evidence right there in his pocket. I pointed to his jeans. "Says the bolt cutters sticking out of your pants."

Now he started to run, dropping the bike and sprinting away. *THWIP!* My webbing quickly latched on to him, and I yanked him back like a yo-yo. I set him against the wall of a nearby building and webbed him to it. He was trapped. I grabbed the bolt cutters from his pocket and— *CRACK*—snapped them in two.

"That should put an end to your bike-burgling days, mister," I told him as he struggled against the web. Now it was time for the applause.

"*Umm*, whose bike is this?" I called out to the people passing by. "Anyone know who locked

their bike up over there? Hello? New York?"
The city's afternoon commuters kept walking. I
turned back to the thief. "Do you have a pen?"

I put the bike back where it was, and then
swung off, but not before leaving a short note: *Is
this your bike? If not, DON'T steal it!—Spider-
Man.* That should do just fine, I told myself, back
on the lookout for any other suspicious-looking
activity.

It wasn't long before I spotted another attempted
robbery, this time some punk trying to jimmy
open a car a few blocks away. Ready—aim—
THWIP! The would-be carjacker was webbed to
the car he was trying to steal.

I landed in front of him. "This stuff is nasty,
yo," he said, trying to peel off the webbing.

I leaned against the car and gave it a little flick,
just enough to set off the car alarm. "Cops'll be

here in a minute," I said casually. My job here done, I was about to swing away when a particularly angry voice came from a window above me.

"Shut that thing off! Who set it off? You, in the red and blue?" A woman was leaning out the window of her apartment above. She seemed pretty unimpressed by my crime-fighting skills.

"This guy was trying to steal—" I started to explain, but she cut me off.

"You idiot; that's *his* car!" she yelled. "He locked his keys inside!" I peeked in. Looked as if she was right.

I looked at the noncarjacking owner and gave a weak shrug. "Well, it did look suspicious. Sorry," I said. "That'll dissolve in a few, um, hours. Did I mention I was sorry?"

Win some, lose some. No one said this would be easy.

It was getting late. Time to check in with HQ.
Plus, I was starving! Swinging up to a higher
perch, I grabbed my sandwich and bit into it as I
pulled out my phone and dialed. The phone rang
a few times on the other end before someone
answered . . . sort of.

Once again, I heard an all-too-familiar voice:
"You've reached the voice mail of Happy Hogan.
You know what to do." The phone beeped. Time
to give a rundown of the day's events.

"Hi, Happy! Here's my report for the night:
Stopped two muggings, one grand theft auto, one
grand theft . . . bicycle. Couldn't find the owner, so
I left a note. I hope he or she got it. Oh, and I
helped a lost old Dominican lady who was really
nice and bought me a churro. But I really think I
could be doing a lot more. Just curious when we're

gonna have our next real mission. Call me back," I finished, about to hang up before remembering one last detail: "It's Peter. Parker."

I hung up. Why did I have to tell him about the churro?

I was almost out of web fluid, so I had to change cartridges. I popped out one, but I fumbled with it, and it fell down to a fire escape landing. No biggie. I jumped down and tried to use my foot to kick it back up into my hand, but it flew away from me instead. I reached out to grab it, stretching out across the fire escape, catching it just before it was out of reach, my feet stuck to the fire escape, body fully extended.

"Well, this is awkward," I said to a pigeon that had watched the whole thing unfold. It just cocked its head to the side, then flew away. I was about to flip back onto the rooftop when I saw … the Hulk?

Okay, obviously it couldn't be the *real* Hulk. I looked again and saw that the guy was only green from the neck up and not nearly as big. And the Hulk wouldn't need to use an ATM like this guy. Hulk mask. ATM booth. Something was definitely fishy about this. Just then, I saw "Hulk" turn and say something to "Iron Man"—again, a cheap mask. Stowing away my half-eaten sandwich, I stood up and was about to swing over when "Iron Man" pulled out the most intense-looking set of bolt cutters I'd ever seen. They were really high-tech! They cut through the ATM with this creepy purple energy beam. I'd never seen anything like it.

Another guy, "Captain America," joined the others and started pulling off the metal casing of the ATM with some sort of antigravity gizmo. It ripped apart the ATM. And finally, "Thor" joined them and started loading cash by the bundle into a large bag.

It seemed the "Avengers" had assembled. And they forgot to invite me.

"Is this a bad time to ask for autographs?" I quipped as I landed a few feet away from them.

My arrival stopped them cold, but that didn't last long. "Hulk" and "Thor" each pulled their weapons out.

"Your 'guns' are supposed to be your muscles, Jolly Green," I said, giving a little arm flex. "And, Thor, you use a hammer, remember?" Ducking quickly, I grabbed the shotgun from "Hulk" and swung it at "Thor's" pistol, disarming them both. "You know, I'm starting to think you guys aren't the real Avengers."

I spotted a desk behind "Hulk" and fired my web. "Hulk" laughed, thinking I'd missed him. *Not so fast, buddy.* I pulled the web back with the desk still attached. It smacked him in the back of the head, knocking him down.

"Oh sorry. I didn't mean to do that so hard," I called.

Out of the corner of my eye, I saw "Cap" start to move his antigravity machine. The chunk of metal he'd ripped open was floating with it.

"What *is* that? And where can I get one?" I asked, webbing the device away from him before he could do something cool like flip a switch and reverse the energy, sending the metal flying my way. "How did you guys end up with tech like this? I mean, no offense, you seem great, but—" The alarm on my watch started to beep. "Curfew time. We should wrap this up."

I flipped over "Thor" and kicked "Cap" hard in the chest, sending him smashing into the ATM. Money started flying everywhere. Whoops— didn't know it was going to do that. I turned my attention back to "Hulk," who was getting back up, wobbling as he tried to stand.

"Stay. Down," I said, jumping off his back and twisting to avoid "Thor," who was taking a swing at me. "So did you guys draw straws for who got which mask? Did everyone fight over Iron Man?"

"Iron Man." I realized I'd almost forgotten about him as I swung "Thor" into the wall.

"Iron Man" was still near the ATM with his crazy bolt cutters. I saw him adjust the settings on the side of the device. Purple energy shot out, slicing the top off the car I had just been perched on. I dodged and darted as the energy beams continued shooting all over. He didn't seem to be able to control it very well. Suddenly, the beam shot across the street right at . . .

"Mr. Dalmar!" I yelled. The purple energy ripped apart Mr. Dalmar's bodega. The noise was making my ears ring as I ran across the street and into the wreckage.

It was a smoky mess inside. *Please, please, let nobody be hurt,* I thought as I entered the rubble. "Mr. Dalmar?" I called out.

A faint voice whimpered weakly at the far end of the store. I rushed over and saw Mr. Dalmar stooped behind the counter.

Putting my hands on his shoulders, I helped him up and out of the store. "Are you okay?" I asked, looking at him in concern.

Mr. Dalmar coughed violently, but he gave me a thumbs-up. Then he turned to look at his now-destroyed bodega and moaned in sorrow. Okay, now this was personal. I turned to finish off the guys who had caused all this and almost killed my friend... But they were gone. No sign of them anywhere at the ATM. *Better let the police handle it from here,* I thought as I heard the sirens approach. Besides, my alarm was going off. Again.

Happy Hogan was working late at Stark Industries when his phone buzzed. He was too focused to pay attention to the caller ID as he answered it.

"Hello?" He was barely giving the call a second thought until he heard the voice on the other side.

"Happy? Boy am I glad you picked up! Listen!" Spider-Man's voice came shouting through the other side. Happy could tell the kid was running and swinging as he talked.

The phone rang a few times, but this time somebody real answered.

"Happy? Boy am I glad you picked up! Listen," I began, trying to contain my excitement as I ran and jumped, but I still ended up shouting. "Something big just happened! These guys were robbing an ATM, and they had these insane weapons and—"

Happy interrupted with an impatient sigh. "Peter, I don't have time for an ATM robbery, or thoughtful notes you leave behind," he said. "I've got higher-priority things to worry about. We're talking important, high-level stuff."

Happy wasn't getting how serious this was.

"But, Happy," I continued, "they had weapons that—"

He interrupted me again: "Just stay away from anything too dangerous. I'm responsible for making sure *you're* responsible. Got it?"

"I *am* responsible! I...Oh!" I trailed off as I turned down the alley where I had webbed my backpack. Except the backpack wasn't there anymore. The entire dumpster was gone. It must have been collected by a garbage truck. Again.

"That doesn't sound responsible," Happy said, his voice sounding fed up.

"I'll call you right back," I said. Maybe the thief hadn't gotten far.

"We'll call you," Happy replied, and promptly hung up on me.

I swung my way home, thinking about my awful day. I had managed to upset Liz, lost my clothes and backpack for the seventh time, let fake Avengers get away with stealing a ton of cash from an ATM, and almost caused Mr. Dalmar to get hurt in the process.

Can this day get any worse? I thought as I arrived at my apartment and crept down from the roof. I opened my window and climbed in onto the ceiling, trying not to let May hear me. She couldn't see me like this.

I quietly flipped down onto the floor and stretched as I removed my mask.

The sound of a thousand pieces of Saturn hitting the floor almost caused me to jump right back out the window.

I wasn't alone.

I saw the pile of blocks around Ned's feet, then I looked up to meet his shocked gaze.

Busted.

CHAPTER 4

"What was that?!"

Great. May was home. This night kept getting more fun.

Ned's mouth moved for about five seconds until his brain caught up with his vocal cords. "You...you're the Spider-Man!" he said. "From the Internet!"

I covered Ned's mouth before he could blurt out my secret identity any louder.

"It was nothing, May!" I yelled, turning my attention back to Ned, while trying my best to laugh the whole thing off. "This? This is just a *costume*. No big deal."

"You were *on the ceiling*!" Ned responded. He wasn't buying it.

Sighing, I pressed the button on my chest, and the suit untightened enough for me to change out of it. No use trying to deny it now. "What are you even doing in here, Ned?!" I asked.

"May let me in," Ned said. "Remember, we were supposed to finish Saturn?" His eyes were still wide open. I don't think he'd blinked yet.

Saturn. Right. Worst timing ever. Just then, the door to my bedroom opened. I shoved the Spidey suit into the closet before May entered.

She looked over the scene in my room and paused. Ned stood over a pile of blocks, while I

61

stood by the closet in nothing but boxers. Worst. Timing. Ever.

PleaseDontAskWhyImNotDressed. PleaseDontAsk WhyImNotDressed.

My mantra paid off! May stared in silence for a few moments before turning to Ned. "Who's up for Thai tonight?" she asked. "Ned? You in?"

"He can't," I answered before he could speak.

"Another time, then," May replied. She glanced at me again, eyebrow crooked. "Maybe you want to put some clothes on, Peter?"

"Yup. Yes. Clothes," I agreed enthusiastically, pushing her out the door. "Getting dressed is next on the agenda. Then Thai. Thanks for checking in, okay, bye."

As soon as the door closed, Ned started with the questions.

"She doesn't know?" he asked.

I pulled on a shirt and said, "No one does.

Except Mr. Stark. He made me the suit, so..." I turned to face Ned. "But listen—"

At the mention of Tony's name, Ned's eyes widened even more. "You're friends with Iron Man?!" he exclaimed, pausing as his brain scrambled to make sense of everything. Then, with a gasp, he asked, "Are you an Avenger?!"

To anyone else, that question might have sounded as ridiculous as asking someone if he were Santa. For me, it was a tiny dagger reminding me that I was not, in fact, an Avenger. "Not officially," I said. "Yet. But soon."

Ned was rapidly pacing around the room now. This was not good. Time to defuse.

"Ned," I started, "you gotta keep this a secret, okay?"

Ned stopped moving mid-step. "A secret?" he asked. "Why?!"

"Ned, people try to kill me every night," I

explained. "Trust me, May's not going to be okay with that."

Ned seemed to think this over for a moment. Then he reached over and grabbed my shoulders, speaking so fast I could hardly understand what he was saying. "Peter, I'm gonna level with you," he said. "There is no way I can keep this a secret. It's the greatest thing that's ever happened to me! My face is so warm right now! I keep this bottled up, I might—"

I twisted and grabbed Ned by his own shoulders, looking him dead in the eye. "Ned. May *cannot* know," I repeated. "Swear it!"

I must have sounded incredibly serious because Ned finally blinked and stepped back a little.

"Okay, I swear," he said, and I knew he meant it. He was still super excited, though. "Can I try on the suit?" he asked. "Is it sticky? Or wait, are *you* sticky?!" The questions would go on all night if I didn't stop them, and I knew May was waiting for dinner.

"I'll explain everything tomorrow. You'll get all the answers, promise," I said, trying to shuttle Ned out as quickly as possible.

Ned stuck his foot in the door before I could close it and peered in. "Wait, one thing: How do you do all of this *and* the Stark internship?"

I pinched the bridge of my nose and sighed. "Ned, there is no internship."

I kicked Ned's foot away and shut the door on his confused look. I counted to three, waiting for him to put the pieces together.

"Ohhhhhhhh!" Ned's voice came through the door right on cue.

I sat on my bed, exhausted both physically from the fight earlier and emotionally from blowing my secret. This must be why the Avengers don't have secret identities.

"Peter, you haven't touched your larb." May's voice pierced through my distracted thoughts. Dinner had been a blur so far. I kept praying May wouldn't ask me about what happened earlier with Ned.

"Do you want pad see ew, instead?" May continued. "I can order you *ew*. How many times do I have to ask you about *ew* before you look up?"

I laughed at her wordplay. She had always been so great with me. I felt a pang of guilt for being so unfocused on our night out. "Sorry," I said. "I just have so much work."

She put her hand on mine on the table. "You sure this internship isn't too much?" she asked. "You never have time to relax or hang out with friends, and you're always so distracted—"

Right then, a newscaster on the small television

in the corner of the restaurant caught my attention. "... a violent confrontation in Queens tonight ... " the reporter was saying, standing by Mr. Dalmar's destroyed bodega.

"Yoo-hoo," I heard May's voice trying to get through to me, but the TV flashed an image from the Battle of New York as the newscaster continued to talk. I saw that same purple energy that came from the weapons those phony Avengers used.

"... involving illicit, alien technology left behind from the battle five years ago," the newscaster explained. "According to the director of the Department of Damage Control, Ann-Marie Hoag, this is the first ... "

It all clicked into place. "The battle," I said. "That's how they did it!" It didn't even occur to me that I was speaking out loud.

"You shouldn't be worrying about that," May

said reassuringly. "You're a teenager. Your biggest problems should be zits and raging hormones."

"May!" I protested, knowing exactly where she was going.

"I'm serious," she said, looking me in the eye. "You shouldn't have to worry about all this on top of an internship."

I met her gaze, trying to be as calm as she was. "I can handle it. Trust me."

She gave me a long look. Was she buying any of this? Then she patted my hand a couple of times and said, "Okay. I do."

She bought it.

"One thing, though," I said, bracing myself for her reaction. "I kinda need another backpack."

May threw her hands up. "What?! That's—"

"Seven. I know. But, I promise, eighth time's the charm."

"How is this even possible?" May asked,

68

sounding slightly exasperated. "Do geniuses know how normal things like backpacks even work?"

"Yes, we are familiar," I replied with a weak smile.

"Unbelievable," she muttered before starting to chuckle, shaking her head. I could only laugh along with her. If she only knew *how* unbelievable it really was...

On the way to the subway for school the next morning, Ned played his own game of Twenty Questions with Spider-Man.

"*That's* how it happened? You got bit by a spider?!" he finally asked after I gave him the whole backstory.

I nodded.

"Makes sense with the name and all, I guess." Then, after thinking it over for a moment, he blurted out, "Can it bite me? Wait, did it hurt?

Oh, whatever, even if it hurt, I'd do it. Probably. How much hurt are we talking?"

"Sorry, man," I said, bursting his spider-dream. "That spider's long dead."

We took a quick detour and walked past Mr. Dalmar's bodega. It looked worse in the daylight. At least Mr. Dalmar was safe. Police tape and what I guessed were Damage Control agents were all around, including one I recognized as Director Hoag from seeing her on TV during dinner.

Looking around, Ned realized I was surveying the area and noticed the concerned look on my face. "Wait, you were here, weren't you?" he asked.

"Yeah."

"Oh man," he said. "You could've died." He patted me on the shoulder for a moment before picking up his interrogation again. "So do you eat flies?"

"What? No!" I looked around to see if anyone heard my outburst. I grabbed Ned's arm and started to walk us toward the subway. "Stop asking so many questions, especially with people around. Someone might hear you."

"Okay. No more questions," he promised. "In public."

That promise lasted until history class.

"*Psst.* Can you communicate with spiders?" Ned whispered. "Are tarantulas cool or mean? You can never tell."

I waved frantically at him to shut up. Ned motioned that his lips were sealed. But they became unsealed in the library during study hall.

"Are all of your senses heightened?" he asked. "Like, can you tell if I showered this morning?"

"Ned! We're in the library!" I said, shushing

him. Thankfully, the bell rang, and I got up and headed to chemistry class. Ned followed. I hoped we'd make it through an entire class without any more questions, but no.

"Do you tend to hide in dark corners? Under sofas and stuff?"

This was getting out of hand. He was my best friend and all, but enough with the questions. Fortunately, gym class was next. We wouldn't be still long enough for him to ask any more questions.

A familiar face was on the CCTV screen in the gym. Coach Wilson was playing Captain America's prerecorded speech about physical fitness. Then Coach started to lead us through the routine. Ned and I started with sit-ups.

"Looking good, Parker," Coach Wilson remarked, somewhat surprised.

Oops! I must have been distracted by all Ned's

questions. I needed to rein it in before anyone else noticed. I slowed down and added the occasional *"Nnnngh"* for good measure. Good thing nobody was paying attention to me—except Ned.

"Whoa, so all this time you've been faking?" Ned gasped. "So that time when the seniors were all picking on me and you stood up and ended up getting your butt kicked, you just let them?!"

"I wish," I said, wincing at the memory. "That was before I got my powers. I was actually trying to win that one."

I turned away from Ned and toward the bleachers, where Betty, Liz, and other upperclassmen were sitting, not paying us any attention. They were playing Kiss, Marry, Kill.

"For me, I'd kiss Thor, marry Iron Man, and kill Hulk," Betty rattled off.

"What about the Spider-Man? He lives right

here in New York. You could get a shot," said Seymour, one of Betty's friends.

"Okay, first, it's just 'Spider-Man,'" Liz corrected. "Did you guys see him on the news last night? He fought off four guys."

"Someone's crushing on Spider-Man," giggled Betty.

Liz blushed. *"Maaaaaaybe."*

"He's probably, like, thirty," Betty said, looking grossed-out at the idea. I wanted to remind her that she'd picked Tony Stark to marry and *he* was even older, but Ned got up before I could react.

Oh no—don't do it, Ned! I tried to beam the thought into his brain. Unfortunately, spiders aren't telepathic. Or at least the one that bit me wasn't.

"Peter knows Spider-Man!" Ned's inexplicable words bounced around the gym in one of those moments where it seemed as if every conversation came to a pause. All eyes were suddenly on me. "They're... they're friends," Ned continued, filling the silence.

A laugh came from behind me. I knew that mocking voice: Flash. Everyone was waiting for me to speak up. Including Liz. I kicked at the floor, unable to meet her curious eyes.

"I sorta know him through my Stark internship," I muttered, before turning to Ned. "I'm not really supposed to talk about it." I was hoping he took the hint.

"Wow, that's actually impressive, Parker," Flash finally said, sounding surprisingly sincere. "You should bring him to Liz's party tonight."

Party? What party? I couldn't just... crash Liz's—

"Yeah, I'm having people over tonight," Liz said, filling in the blanks. "You're totally welcome to come if you want."

"It'll be dope!" Flash said. "And if you got Spider-Man to come with you? Real cred, Parker." He was definitely trying to call my bluff. Liz glared at him.

"It's okay; I know Peter's too busy for things like parties anyway," she said, sounding slightly...sad?

Before I could answer, the bell rang and everyone started to exit. I hung back with Ned until everyone else was gone. "What are you trying to do?" I hissed. "You almost—"

"Helped you out? I know." He grinned. "You're welcome, by the way."

I was lost. "Helped me?"

Ned sighed and pointed to where Liz had been sitting. "Weren't you listening?" he said. "Liz has a crush on Spider-You!"

My face flushed. Maybe a party could be fun. "I guess I could ask Mr. Stark for the night off."

"Right—the internship," Ned replied, nodding

in understanding. He had apparently forgotten what I'd told him the night before.

"Ned, there's no internship. It was my—"

"Your cover! That's right! I meant to tell you, totally sold everyone on that," Ned said. "You think fast on your feet, Pete. That'll come in handy tonight when we...par-tay!" He tried a little jig as he spoke. He was even worse at dancing than keeping secrets.

CHAPTER 5

"**T**his was a mistake. Let's just go home."

My nerves were starting to get the better of me as we pulled up to Liz's house. A flood of upper-classmen streamed in and out of the house, and my heart raced. I tugged at my sleeve to cover up my Spidey suit underneath.

"Are you kidding me?" May said, looking up at the house from the driver's seat. "Go in there and have fun. Just don't let any girls pressure you into anything you don't—"

"I get it, I get it," I said. She was trying to embarrass me. And it was working.

I followed Ned out of the car as May continued her hilarious "parenting advice," and the two of us walked up to the house. The music was thumping in my chest, and everywhere I looked I saw people much, much cooler than me and Ned hanging out. We froze just inside the doorway, Ned fingering his ridiculous fedora, while I kept tugging at my shirtsleeve.

"I can't believe you guys are at this lame party." Michelle's voice startled me. Looking down, I saw her in a chair, reading a book as if she were in the loudest library on earth.

"You're here, too," I shot back.

"Am I?" Michelle replied, looking at me for a

moment before going back to her book. Man, she could be seriously weird sometimes.

"Hey, guys!" I heard Liz call out. "Welcome!"

"You too," I said before I realized how silly it sounded. "Welcome back, I mean." *C'mon, Parker, find your words!* "I mean, thanks for the invite." *Whew.*

Ned was gawking at all the people crammed into the house. "Sick house!" he said. "I can't believe your parents let you have a party in here!"

Liz blushed slightly. "Yeah, my parents feel guilty working all the time," she said, glancing at me. "You guys would really get along, Peter." Her joke hit a little close to home, and I looked down a little. Liz laughed. "That's it! That's the same guilty look they give me!"

I chuckled nervously, and then there was a moment of silence between us. Super awkward. I finally opened my mouth to speak, when a shattering sound came from the other room.

Looking over her shoulder as she went to investigate, Liz gave a big grin and said, "I better go check on that. I'm really glad you guys came!"

"Dude, this is your chance," Ned whispered after she left. "Just have Spider-Man swing in and say hi. Oh, and if he can also give me a fist bump that would be—"

I cut Ned off. "This is stupid. Spider-Man isn't a party trick," I said a little too aggressively to cover the fact that I was starting to have cold feet about the whole thing. Then I heard a voice behind me that warmed them back up.

"Hey, Parker!" Flash said. "Where's your buddy, Spider-Man? Let me guess: He blew you off to go fight crime. *Sorry*, bud." His sarcastic tone made my face flush as he walked off with his friends, all of them laughing. Looking across the room, I saw Liz glancing over at us with . . . was that pity?

Okay. Enough.

"Cover me," I told Ned, sneaking upstairs and out a bathroom window.

It was chilly out as I took off my clothes and webbed them high in a tree behind Liz's house. I pulled on my mask and pressed the chest button to tighten the suit.

"Hey, guys, just swinging by to say 'Hi' to my best bros Ned and Peter," I said, practicing my best Super Hero voice.

This was ridiculous. I sighed and reached for my clothes to get dressed.

A loud, booming sound stopped me as I was about to put one leg in my pants. Standing up on the roof, I scanned the horizon to locate where the sound had come from. Holy crap. It was that purple-energy thing again! Its trail was still arching across the sky.

Okay, Fake-vengers—time for Round Two.

A few miles away, under an abandoned bridge, I tucked my body into a dark hiding place, trying to figure out what the heck was going on. Below me, a few men stood behind an unmarked van.

Apparently, one of them was named Brice, or at least that's what the others called him. He held a piece of tech that looked familiar—like the one I'd seen in the ATM fight. From this angle, I swear it looked like an Ultron arm from the attack in Sokovia!

"I got a ton of great stuff in here, right, Schultz?" Brice said, opening the back of the van. "Take a look, man—RF cloners, black-hole grenades, stun batons, antigravity climbers…"

What I could see in the back of the van was

equal parts impressive and terrifying. Theirs were definitely the wrong hands for this kind of stuff. Time for me to—

BREEET BREEET BREEET!

Dang it! Super Hero 101: Always put your phone on vibrate when stalking bad guys.

"What was that?" Brice asked, looking around. Welp, my cover was blown. No use trying to hide anymore. I jumped down a few feet away from the van.

"Uh, stop. I am the law and you're under arrest," I called out, trying not to let on how much I was sweating under my suit.

"You set us up!" Schultz yelled, pulling out his gun.

I quickly webbed the gun to his hand. "If you're gonna shoot at somebody, shoot at me," I said.

KA-BLAMO. Out of nowhere, the Brice guy punched me with some kind of gauntlet, sending me about ten feet in the air. Guess I asked for that.

Brice and Schultz raced inside the van, as the one they called Alex ran to his car. Groggily, I got to my feet as they started their engines. "I'm Spider-Man!" I said. They revved up. "Guys?" Clearly, they weren't listening. Enough talk. Time for action.

THWIP! THWIP! I webbed both the car and the van at the same time, and pulled as hard as I could. The back car window came flying off, and I had to duck from getting smacked. I stood up—only to be yanked back down as the van took off, with me doing the worst water-skiing impression ever as it pulled me along behind it.

I held on as the van turned one corner and then another. Raising my head, I saw Brice grab a weapon from the back of the van and aim it right at me. The purple power core lit up just as he pulled the trigger. At that moment, the van turned another corner, and Brice lost his footing, the weapon flying out of his hands as it blasted wildly. I ducked, and it missed me, but it tore open the side of the van and then hit my webbing, sending me sprawling away from the van.

No, no, no! These guys were not going to get away from your friendly neighborhood Spider-Man again! Except...I was stuck literally in a neighborhood. No tall buildings to swing from. *Time to improvise,* I thought, leaping over fences, past dogs, through a backyard campout *(Hi, kids; no time for autographs, sorry. Please stop screaming.)*, and—oh cool—a trampoline. Bouncing as high as I could, I saw the van a few streets over.

I ran as fast as I could toward the intersection, praying they were headed in the same direction.

Swinging down from a lamppost at the intersection, I saw the van and breathed a sigh of relief...before realizing that it was heading straight at me. Thinking fast, I flipped onto the top of the van. All I had to do was crawl to the front and—

Whoa! I was suddenly about twenty feet higher! The wind was whooshing in my ears as I looked up to see what had plucked me from the van. It was...some kind of flying creature? All I could really make out were a set of glowing eyes and an enormous wingspan as we continued to rise higher and higher. Trying not to look down, I wondered whether I could survive a fall from this height. Mr. Demon Wings didn't seem to care either way.

A beeping noise caught us both off guard. It was coming from my suit! Next thing I knew, a parachute exploded from my back, tearing me away from the flying monster. He started to dive down, and in my panic to get away from him, I got tangled in the lines. Looking up, I caught a quick glimpse of the creature backlit against the moon. His massive wings and bright eyes were the last thing I saw before—

SPLASH! Hitting the water felt like being slammed into a building. Better to fall into the lake than onto the ground, I suppose. I tried swimming up, but I kept getting caught in the parachute until I was tangled up like, well, a fly in a spiderweb. *Fitting demise,* I thought, as the last of the air in my lungs went bubbling up to the rapidly vanishing surface.

I felt myself go deeper...

Deeper...

With a muted *THUNK,* I hit the bottom of the lake. The last thing I remembered before my vision faded was the glow of the demon's eyes, getting brighter and brighter.

Yup. This was it. This was the end.

CHAPTER 6

I gasped for air as I broke through the surface of the water. I wasn't dead! Hooray! I looked up to see who—or what—was carrying me, and again I saw the glow of inhuman eyes. But these eyes were different, more familiar to me somehow. And this creature didn't have wings, but it *did* have propulsion jets that reminded me of...

Iron Man!

I'd been rescued!

We landed next to the lake, and I started talking as fast as I could through chattering teeth, explaining to Iron Man what had happened.

"And then this flying guy grabbed me—he looked like a monster!" I said, willing myself to play it cool, as if I were an Avenger who saw things like these every day. "I mean, I wasn't scared. I knew he obviously wasn't a monster."

Iron Man stood, unmoving. "And then this unscary not-monster dropped you in the lake?" he asked, a hint of sarcasm in his voice.

Well, technically, it was the parachute in my suit, but I didn't want to seem ungrateful. "Why is there a parachute in this thing?" I asked. "I don't need a parachute."

"Clearly," he responded drily.

"How'd you even find me?" I asked. Then it

dawned on me. No way. He didn't… "Did you put a tracker in my suit?!"

"Yes, and it's *my* suit," he corrected me. "You're leasing it at a monthly don't-get-yourself-killed rate. There's a heater, too," he stated, noticing my shivering. He touched a sensor on my suit, and it was like being dry-cleaned in seconds, steam rising around me. It felt amazing.

"*Ooooh*. That's cool—er, hot." I straightened up a little and put on my best "playing it cool" voice. "I was fine, by the way. You didn't have to come all the way out here—"

"Oh, I'm not here," Iron Man replied, as his visor popped open to reveal nothing inside. No Tony Stark inside. Nothing.

"Um, your suit's… empty."

"There's about three million dollars of tech in that suit. That's not empty." He was right on a technicality.

"So where are you?" I asked, looking around suspiciously. I half expected to see a drone in the sky spying on me.

"India," came the response. "I thought I'd hit up a Hindu temple. Center myself. That sort of thing." *Wow,* I thought. *I guess when you have Stark money, you can do stuff like that.* "Thank God this place has Wi-Fi or you would have drowned."

"I had a strategy." I did not have a strategy.

"What, to die and fight him in the afterlife?"

"Don't you see?" I pressed, getting a little frustrated. "He's the source of the weapons. Chitauri, Sokovia. I gotta find him and take him down!"

I could feel his eyes roll all the way from India. *"Take him down?"* Tony said. "Easy, junior. Best to just stay out of it and let the people who handle this sort of thing do their jobs."

"Who is that?" I asked. "The Avengers? I can help!" This could be my shot.

"Just trust me. Stay out of it."

"But why?" I whined. When was he going to take me seriously?

"Because I said so." The Iron Man suit put its hand on the side of its head in frustration. "I really don't want to sound like my old man here. Look, kid, just forget the flying man. Stay closer to the ground in Queens, build up your game helping the little people. You know, like the old lady who bought you that churro."

That churro. Happy had told him everything. "Look, Tony—uh, Mr. Stark," I started, "I'm done with the ground. I'm ready for the next level."

"Really?" he replied. "Because it looks like a mysterious flying guy almost drowned you."

"How much longer do I have to wait?" I asked,

wondering if there was a minimum-age requirement to be an Avenger.

"Have you thought about where you're going to college?"

"College?!" That was, like, ten years away in Super Hero time.

"Good-bye, Peter. Say hi to your hot aunt for me."

"But—" I reached out to grab the suit, but he was already gone.

"Mr. Stark is no longer connected," a monotone voice reported. The suit fired up the boot repulsors and flew off. He'd hung up on me.

Stay on the ground. Was that supposed to be funny? Wait a minute! The ground! I swung back over to the bridge. Something was gnawing at the back of my mind. I remembered the van turning a corner, and Brice losing his footing, causing his weapon to fall somewhere around...

"There!" I yelped. My hopes were dashed a little when I saw that the weapon had been smashed to bits. But what was this? A purple glowy egg thing? Bingo.

Hey, I thought as I swung back to grab my clothes from Liz's and head home, *it was on the ground when I found it. Just following orders.*

"Thanks for bailing on me. Didn't you get my messages?" Ned's voice startled me.

"Sorry; I got carried away," I replied, half smiling at my own joke. Before he could respond, I moved aside and showed him what I was working on.

Bam! Bam! I'd finally found a use for shop class. I banged on the egg thing in the back of the room, trying to crack it open.

"Whoa," Ned said, his eyes nearly popping out of his head. "What is it?"

"Dunno." I shrugged. "But some guy tried to vaporize me with it last night."

"Seriously? That's so awesome," Ned said before seeing the look on my face. "I mean, not awesome in the almost-dying way, but awesome in the whole blaster way. It *is* a blaster, right?"

"Yeah, I think this is the energy source. It looks alien. Chitauri probably."

Ned looked closer. "Almost like a battery," he muttered. "But it's attached to microprocessors. And look, that's a solid-state relay like I use for internal computer fans."

Ned was way better than me when it came to computer stuff. I knew one thing, though: "Someone built this weapon combining alien tech with ours."

"That is literally the coolest sentence anyone has ever said!" Ned yelled, his mind officially blown.

For the rest of class, we tried everything possible to crack open the battery, but it wouldn't give. Finally, I tried brute force to pull it apart. At first, it wouldn't budge. Then, with a *POP*, it came loose. Score!

Next thing I knew, a flare of purple energy nearly singed my eyebrows! Ned looked around while I checked to make sure all my face was still in its proper place.

"Clear," he whispered.

I shoved the battery and the rest of the tech into my backpack as the bell rang. "I gotta figure out what this thing is and who made it," I said. Ned cleared his throat. "Right, *we* gotta do it. Meet me after school?"

"Duh," Ned replied. Obviously, he would never miss out on something like this.

We made our way to the physics lab after everyone had cleared out. The battery was still glowing slightly, but there were no more purple bursts. If we could just figure out what made it tick...

"First, I say we put that glowy thing in the mass spectrometer," Ned said, thinking out loud.

"Before that, let's come up with a better name for it than 'glowy thing,'" I suggested.

We were trying to think of a slightly cooler name when I realized we weren't alone. Peering down the hall, I noticed something moving. Two big somethings—somebodies, actually. One of the two men looked familiar: He was one of the goons from last night! Schultz, I think they called him. Some other flunky was following him. Schultz was looking intently at some gizmo in his hands. My stomach sank, and I shoved Ned back into the classroom.

"That's one of the guys who tried to kill me," I said, looking at Ned.

Ned paled. "What?!" he whispered loudly. "We should leave. Like, leave the state! Or, at least, the school!" He started hyperventilating.

"Wait." I stopped him. "Maybe they can lead me to the guy who dropped me in the lake."

"Someone dropped you in a lake? *Ohhh*, so that's how you got 'carried away.'" he said, putting everything together. He looked at me nervously. "Y'know, that's the kind of detail you shouldn't leave out."

I could hear Schultz's voice getting closer: "This thing says it was some kind of energy pulse."

"Whatever it is, it's gone now, Schultz," replied the lowlife who was with him.

Schultz's voice became deadly serious. "The name's Shocker now, remember?"

Well, that was new.

"Whatever it was, it's gone now, *Shocker*," the other goon said.

"Yeah. So are we," I whispered to Ned as we both turned to escape in the other direction. A loud clang sounded as Ned tripped on one of the chairs in the room. I turned to see Shocker and his accomplice heading right for us.

Great. Trapped in school with a super villain and my best friend. I braced myself for Round Three.

CHAPTER 7

I shoved Ned under the teacher's desk and leaped onto the ceiling just as the door opened and Shocker entered. He looked around, but not up, thankfully.

"Whatever. Let's get outta here. The boss'll be wanting a report," he said.

As Shocker turned to leave, I managed to fire a Spidey tracer from my wrist cartridge onto his pants. The nanobug scurried down his pants and into a seam. Two could play at the secret tracking game.

"What was that?!" Ned whispered after they left.

"Come over to my place and I'll show you," I replied.

Later, back in my room, I showed Ned a holographic projection of the city beaming from my web shooter. A bright-red dot was moving across the map.

"You're tracking him?" Ned asked. "Ha! The hunter becomes the hunted, sucker." He couldn't take his eyes off the map. "Look, they're leaving Brooklyn."

We waited and watched.

"Now Staten Island," Ned observed.

More time crawled by, and the map moved with it. My butt was getting numb sitting there watching, but Ned couldn't get enough. "Leaving Jersey!" he continued.

Jersey? Where were these guys going? And how was I supposed to catch them if they were in—

"There, they stopped," Ned said suddenly.

"Culpeper, Virginia?" I was stumped. "How the heck am I supposed to track them down to their—"

"Evil lair. Just say it…for me." Ned was far more excited than I was as I raced through ways to follow them.

"Fine." I relented. "How am I supposed to get to their evil lair three hundred miles away?" I flopped onto the bed. Virginia. I looked at the map again, an idea forming. "Hey, Ned, Culpeper doesn't look too far from DC, does it?"

Ned smiled, and I knew he was thinking the same thing. "Oh man. Liz is gonna kill you."

The entire decathlon team was filing onto the bus the next morning as I raced up to hand my permission slip to Mr. Harrington, the team's coach.

Liz was standing outside the bus, clipboard in hand, double-checking that everyone was there. She looked at me, puzzled. "Peter?"

Aboard the bus, Ned waved, probably a little too enthusiastically. "Hey, buddy!" he called out.

I stuttered and fumbled my way back onto the decathlon team—which ended up not being too hard since they still needed me for the physics portion—much to Flash's aggravation.

"No way!" he objected. "You can't just quit on us and then turn around and stroll up here and—"

"Flash," Liz cut him off, her voice leaving no doubt as to who the captain was.

A bored voice came from the back of the bus. "Can we leave already?" Michelle asked. "I was hoping to get in some light protesting outside one of the embassies before dinner."

Liz smiled at me as I took my seat.

Don't blush. Don't blush.

I blushed and gave a small smile back as I settled in next to Ned for the trip to Washington, DC.

As we approached our nation's capital, Liz led the team in a lightning round of quiz questions. But my mind was elsewhere. Culpeper, Virginia, to be exact. I didn't know what I would find there, but it probably wasn't going to be good. My phone buzzed, breaking my thoughts. Blocked number? That could mean only one thing.

"Hello?" I knew who was on the other end before he even spoke.

"Got a little blip on my screen here." Happy Hogan was fishing for information, and he didn't sound amused. "You left New York?"

Huh? How did he—the tracker! "It's just a school trip," I said, whispering. "And I gotta say,

Happy, tracking me without my permission? Not cool. It's a complete violation of my privacy. Is this the kind of world you want to live in?" Ned glanced at me, and I remembered that we were doing the same thing. *This is different,* I mouthed to Ned.

"What was that?" Happy asked. I forgot he was still on the line.

"Uh, nothing. Just some kid on the bus." I covered. "Look, we're just going to DC for the Academic Decathlon. No big deal."

Happy grunted. "I'll decide if it's a big deal." Long pause. Really long pause. Finally, his internal deliberation concluded, Happy gave his verdict. "It seems like no big deal. Just be careful. Someone once stole my sister's camera in DC."

"Okay, got it. Eyes on my camera-that-I-didn't-bring at all times." We hung up, and I mentally kicked myself. Stupid tracker.

I was still trying to figure out how to get around the tracker in my suit when we pulled up to the hotel.

The rest of the team enthusiastically pointed out how amazing the place was as we checked in.

"It's, like, where God would stay if he were in town!" Ned exclaimed.

I looked at him, gazing in wonder, and got an idea. It was time to improvise.

"Ned, I'm gonna need your help," I whispered. In an instant, Ned's fascination with the hotel faded as he saw me pat the bag holding my Spidey suit.

"Best. Field. Trip. Ever." Ned grinned.

With the DO NOT DISTURB sign hanging on our door, I unpacked the suit and turned it inside out. It was tricked out with electronic wiring, circuit boards, armor—probably your average, run-of-the-mill fare for Tony Stark. I unpacked the glowy thing (still needed a better name) and put it on the bed, too, as Ned fiddled with the wires until he found a way to plug it into his laptop.

I brought the hologram map back up. Shocker hadn't left Culpeper. Good.

"*Sooooo* why are we removing the tracker from your suit?" Ned asked.

"Because I need to follow these guys to their boss before they move again," I explained for the hundredth time. "And I don't want Mr. Stark to know."

Ned looked nervous. "So we're lying to Iron Man?!"

"We're not *lying*," I said. "We're just not telling him. He doesn't know what I can do yet."

Ned found the tracker in my suit and pulled it out. I set it on the nightstand and watched the flashing red dot on his laptop monitor. Looked like "Spider-Man" wouldn't be leaving the hotel room for some time.

Ned whistled in awe as he continued to fiddle with the suit. "Whoa. Did you know there's a ton of other subsystems in this thing? But they're disabled by the..." He pointed at the monitor and chuckled.

I read the file name and groaned. "Training Wheels Protocol? Seriously?" *They aren't taking me seriously,* I thought. Only one way to prove them wrong. "Ned, can you turn the protocol off?"

"*Yeahhhh,*" Ned said, hesitantly. "But I don't think it's a good idea. They're probably blocked for a good reason."

I didn't have time to argue. "I can handle it, Ned. Just trust me."

With a heavy sigh, Ned typed in code for

what seemed like an eternity, and suddenly the diagnostics of the suit started to light up in green.

A *BEEP* came from the computer. The screen flashed PROTOCOL DISABLED. I smiled. Suddenly, the suit twitched on the bed, and I nearly jumped onto the ceiling.

"*Ummm*, when I put it on, it's not going to explode or anything, will it?" I asked.

Ned shrugged. "Training Wheels are off, Spidey. My job here is finished."

"Actually, not yet," I said, turning to the other object on the bed. "Glowy thing. It's evidence. Keep it safe."

Ned stuffed it into his backpack. "As long as you keep yourself safe."

I sneaked out of the room and checked the holographic map. Still no movement. Good.

I was about to open the exit door when a voice stopped me.

"Sneaking out?" Busted.

It was Liz. I turned, expecting to see a disapproving look. Instead, she was smiling. "Don't worry; we all are. *Shhhh*—I arranged with the hotel for a little night swimming in the pool. Everyone else thinks I swiped the card from housekeeping."

"Going for the good-girl-gone-bad trophy?" I joked.

She blushed. "A stress-relieving team activity is beneficial before competition, and teenagers respond to things they perceive as breaking the rules," she said, sounding as though she was reciting. "I read a coaching book."

"Sounds like fun," I said, looking toward the pool longingly, "but I was just gonna get some air. The bus wiped me out." I hated lying—and missing out on swimming with Liz—but Shocker and his goons might not be in Culpeper much longer.

"As team captain, I order you to have fun," Liz said in a playfully commanding voice. Any other day, I would have obeyed.

Dumb bad guys.

BEEP. Crap. The baddies were on the move! "Liz, I would love to—"

"Then do," she said, grabbing my hand. "Just for a bit."

Another *BEEP.* "I . . . I can't." I pulled my hand away, anxious to catch the villains before they vanished, but I think I pulled too hard, judging by the look on Liz's face.

Just great.

"Fine," she said. "You're not the only one who's stressed, Peter. You don't have to be weird." She turned toward the pool door. "Team breakfast at seven. Don't be late," she stated, not looking back.

If only I could tell her...

Up on the roof, I glanced down at the team having fun in the pool while I changed into my suit. I pulled on the mask, and suddenly it sparked to life. There were crazy readouts, biometrics, maps. I wondered if this was what it was like being inside Iron Man's head.

"Good evening, Peter," a female voice came from inside my mask. I almost fell back. "Where would you like to take me tonight?"

My suit was asking me out? No, idiot. It was probably a guidance program. Training Wheels were off, remember. "Uh, well, I was gonna go here." I pointed at the moving tracker.

"It would be my pleasure to direct you, Peter," said my suit (this would take getting used to).

"*Ummmm*, thank you, uh...ma'am," I said,

hoping my suit didn't think I was a complete dork.

The display in my mask lit up and zoomed in on a truck. "That vehicle is projected to go in the direction you have requested."

That was all I needed to hear. Swinging from the hotel marquee, I flipped onto the rumbling semitruck. May always warned me never to hitchhike. I bet she never pictured something like this. Heck, I never imagined I'd be doing anything like this! I was in unchartered waters now. Anything could happen.

CHAPTER 8

"**O**ne hundred meters from target and closing, Peter."

I didn't know if I would ever get used to my suit talking to me. And it was a *she*?! Anyway, whatever. Finally, after being on top of this truck for almost an hour, it was showtime.

"Okay," I said, leaping off the truck. I tucked and rolled as I hit the ground. According to the hologram map, the bad guys were just over the hill in front of me.

As I crested the hill, I saw a rusted, abandoned gas station. A beat-up van was parked alongside it. The lackey I'd seen at school was behind the wheel, and Shocker was on watch next to him with night-vision binoculars. Some guy I had never seen before was messing with some equipment, and I could hear random radio chatter coming from whatever he was working on.

"Mason," Shocker said to the man. "Tinkerer, anything?" The man looked up and shook his head no.

Huh. Curiouser and curiouser. "What are they doing?" I wondered aloud.

I jumped a little when my suit answered. "I do not know. Should I engage Enhanced Combat Mode?"

"Um, sure. Sounds cool." I was a fan of anything

my suit could do that was "enhanced." I started to make my way closer to the gas station when … Yikes! My mask lit up like Christmas! Things started zooming in and out, magnifying and converting to infrared.

I started to stumble around blindly. "Whoa, whoa, whoa!" Suddenly, I was tripping over rusted pipes and smacking into a gas pump. "Not so bright!" I said in a hushed voice. My vision went back to normal.

I waited for a long moment, convinced everyone from here to DC had heard me. Nothing.

CREAK. The sound of the van's door opening made me wonder if my cover had been blown. Peering around the pump, I saw Shocker heading in my direction. Yup, cover blown. He pulled out a crazy gun that looked as if it had been modified with alien technology. No telling what that thing could do. I knew I had to swing away fast. I shot a web from my left hand to the top of the gas station and . . .

It split in two?!

"Enhanced Combat Mode. Your left shooter fires splitter webs," my suit explained. *Now she tells me.* Shocker was unfazed. If anything, it made him start to charge faster. Okay, right hand, same spot. BINGO! But then . . .

ZAP! Electricity ran through the webbing! The old, abandoned station glowed for a moment, as if I had lit it up for the Fourth of July. Then everything went dark again.

"What the—?!"

My ever helpful suit belatedly told me, "And your right fires taser webs."

Maybe I did need some Training Wheels after all. "Just . . . un-enhance! De-hance!" I wished I knew the magic word to make the suit go less crazy.

"Terminating Enhanced Combat Mode," the suit announced. Huh, well that worked.

I saw Shocker coming closer, so I swung behind a busted-up car, fired a web at a hanging sign, and started pulling. It swung noisily back and forth. Distracted by it, Shocker changed direction. Ha! Sucker. He lit the area with a flashlight, but all he saw was a rusty, old sign swaying in the wind. He went back to the van.

I had to get closer to hear what they were saying. The guy he called Tinkerer perked up and spoke into a microphone hooked around his ear. "Bogey inbound."

"I got visual," Shocker confirmed.

I looked down one side of the road and up the other. About a mile away, I spotted their "bogey"— a cargo truck headed right into their trap.

"Bogey confirmed," Tinkerer said into his mic. "Green light, green light, Toomes."

Whatever was happening, it was about to go down any second. But why that truck? What could they—oh no, there it was!

Swooping down from the sky was the winged monster from the lake. I barely registered Shocker saying, "Vulture, inbound." So the demon had a name.

The Vulture flew down until he was hovering just above the truck. He dropped some sort of device onto the roof. They were close enough now for me to see that the top of the cargo truck was vanishing!

As the truck came closer, I swung onto the trailer and peeked into where the top had been. The Vulture was sifting through the cargo until he found what he was looking for: alien tech. He started to stash it in a bag. Okay, I'd seen enough. Time to spring my surprise.

THWIP! I webbed his hand to his side, "clipping" his wing.

"Hey," I said, waving. "Remember me?"

The next thing I knew, his other wing was swinging around, knocking my feet off the floor. He pulled out a huge knife and started to charge at me. Instinctively, I kicked at him. Hard. The Vulture went flying through the nonexistent roof. I started to lunge after him, but his wing knocked the device he'd used on the roof earlier, and in a second, the opening was gone. Unable to change course, I slammed headfirst into the ceiling.

Okay, we have to stop meeting like this, I thought, just as I started to black out...

Bump. Thump. Slam. The sounds of metal hitting against metal woke me up. My head was pounding, and I could feel a giant bump on my forehead.

I was stuck in some kind of cargo container. But it wasn't moving. Wherever it was going, the delivery had been made. Or maybe we were stuck at a very long traffic light.

I looked at the ceiling of the container. Maybe…if I…*pushed*…

Guh. Nothing. No give at all.

"How did he do that?" I muttered. How does a hole appear and then become solid again?!

"Analysis determines it was some type of hybrid alien phasing technology," my suit answered.

"I don't suppose I have a setting for phasing webs, do I?"

"No."

Thanks a lot, Suit-Lady.

I looked at the heaps of junk all around me. "What is all this stuff?"

The suit didn't take long to inventory my surroundings. "It appears to be debris from an area where alien or other exotic technology was used."

Then it hit me. "So that's how he gets it; he steals from these guys. Question is, who *are* these guys?"

I climbed over to the ventilation holes on the side of the container and peered through. A giant sign read DEPARTMENT OF DAMAGE CONTROL.

My throat tightened. "What? Damage Control?! No, no, no, I can't be in here!"

My suit agreed. "It does seem unwise. Trespassers are prosecuted. Or shot."

"It's worse than that—if they find me in here, Mr. Stark is gonna kill me!" I started to panic. I had to get out of here!

I peeped outside again. "Is the coast clear?" I whispered.

"I am not detecting any life-forms," the suit replied.

Okay, there was a door at the end of the container. All I had to do was push…hard…er…est. Nothing. Maybe a running start…

WHOOF! I slammed into the door. It didn't even dent.

"Come on!" I complained, sitting down, defeated, not knowing what to do. I'd gone over everything a dozen times. I was stuck.

But not alone.

"I feel bad calling you 'Suit-Lady,'" I said to my AI companion. "Should I give you a name? What about Karen?"

Nothing.

I flopped down and tried to get comfortable as the minutes turned into hours. Finally, after trying to re-create the New York skyline out of junk, something hit me. I started rummaging around.

"Maybe there's something in here I could use. That Vulture guy didn't look like he was done dumpster-diving when I surprised him."

The mask's eyes narrowed as the suit scanned the area. "There." It lit up an object buried about a foot below me. Score! I started digging, and shortly after, I knew I had found it.

"A glowy thing!" It was just like the one Ned and I cracked open.

"A Chitauri energy source," the suit explained. "Commonly found after the Battle of New York."

This was perfect. If I could pull it apart like the last one and aim it at the door . . .

The suit interrupted my great escape plan. "If damaged, the energy source will emit a pulse," she said.

"Yeah, I know," I replied.

"Eventually it will purge all of its energy," the suit finished.

Purge all its… "You mean, like, explode?!"

"The blast could damage the door, if that is your train of logic. However, in this confined space, you might be killed."

The glowy thing was a ticking time bomb once cracked, I realized. Ned and I had already cracked one open, which meant only one thing…

I had left an alien bomb with… "Ned!"

CHAPTER 9

Okay, was it time to panic yet? I had to warn Ned that the Chitauri-energy-source-alien-battery thing could go off at any moment. My best friend...Liz...the entire decathlon team... they were all in danger.

And, of course, I had no cell service. Of course.

I pounded on the door of the container, but it wouldn't give. Turning in frustration, I sifted through the rubble and found some concrete blocks I could use as a brace. Wedging my back against them, I put my feet on the door and pressed as hard as I could. My thighs were burning, but I didn't care. I...had...to...get... this...door...

CRACK! The door flew off its hinges and hurled across the room.

"YES!" I shouted. I was—

Not free. At all. I was surrounded by concrete walls. There were no windows, only a door ten times as massive as the one I'd just barely broken free from. "Seriously?" I wondered. "What's going on?"

"You are in some kind of storage vault," my suit replied. "The walls are solid concrete, and that door is three feet thick."

"Okay, sorry, Mr. Stark." I sighed. "I know you said to keep a low profile, but I gotta get out!" I started banging on the door, but it only echoed through the room. My shouts for help bounced off the walls. I had given everything I had just to get out of that container. The suit was no help, and I was stuck, waiting.

What must have been several hours later, I heard the door finally start to groan. It was opening! I leaped onto the wall above the door and sneaked out over the workmen's heads as they entered. I had to act fast before they noticed—

"Uh, guys..." said one of the workmen, pointing to the torn-off door of the container.

It didn't take long for the alarms to start blaring and the gates to shut. I raced out of the room as fast as I could before the whole facility went on lockdown. Swinging over a fence on the outer perimeter, I landed on top of a truck carrying big concrete tubes. Pulling up my holo-map, I checked to see if the truck was headed toward DC. It was. And I had service bars on my phone again!

"Pick up, Ned! *PickUpPickUpPickUp!*" I yelled into my phone. Where could he be?

"Peter?" I finally heard Ned answer. I'd never been so happy to hear his voice. "Are you okay? You missed the decathlon!"

"Yeah, I was a little, um, stuck," I said. "Ned, I need you to focus. Where is the glowy thing?" Every second counted. I had to know that he was far away from it in case—

"Don't worry, it's safe," Ned whispered back. Okay, safe was good. "I've got it in my backpack." *Not* good!

"What?! Ned where are you?"

"We're at the Washington Monument," he informed me. Great. Huge public space full of people. "Michelle is having some sort of sit-in and won't go inside, but, Peter, you need to—"

"Ned! Listen!" I cut him off. "You have to—"

The rest of my sentence was lost in some fumbling on the other end, and I heard Liz telling Ned to "hand it over."

"Peter, is that you?" Liz asked. She was not happy.

"Liz? Listen, I—"

"You flake!" she continued. "You're lucky we won anyway or I would—"

I definitely wasn't listening. There wasn't time. "Liz," I began, "I—"

She interrupted me again, this time sounding concerned. "I want to be mad, but I'm really more worried, honestly. I mean, what is going on with you? You were weird last night, and nobody could find you today. Level with me: Is it drugs? That would explain a lot."

Drugs? No.

Bad guys with alien tech? Yes.

But I couldn't explain that to her. "Liz, listen to me!"

"Peter, we're going through security," she said before I could go on. "I gotta hang up. But you're in big trouble. Mr. Harrington is not happy."

Then the line went dead.

"Liz? Liz!" *Shoooooot.* I tried dialing again, but Ned wasn't picking up his phone, and time was running out. "Suit-Lady, scan the area for the fastest way to the Washington Monument!"

I pictured Ned's backpack making its way down the security conveyer belt. Would the security guard notice something suspicious, or would he just pass them off as a bunch of high-school geeks?

Was the Chitauri battery starting to glow and pulse yet? Would anyone notice Ned's bag turning purple? Or would they all be transfixed on oohing and aahing at the "world's tallest obelisk"?

Finally! I could see the Washington Monument! I leaped off the tour bus I'd been clinging to for the past however-long. Looking up, I saw the feet of Giant Abraham Lincoln. A *loooooooong* rectangular pool separated me from the Washington Monument. Where were lampposts and tall buildings when you needed them? Only one choice: run!

I sprinted along the pool toward the giant obelisk, but it didn't seem to get any closer. "How long *is* this thing?" I groaned.

"The Lincoln Memorial Reflecting Pool is two thousand and twenty—"

"Wasn't really asking, suit!" I said. I needed to lighten my load, so I hurled my backpack into a tree and webbed it there for safekeeping.

About two thousand and twentysomething feet later, I finally reached the base of the Washington Monument, only to almost trip over Michelle.

"Um," I said in my Super Hero voice. "Where's your class?"

Michelle looked at me in shock and pointed up.

How far up they were was what I needed to know. Suddenly, I had my answer, in the form of my worst fear.

FWA-BOOM!

A stream of purple energy lit up and burst out of the top of the Washington Monument.

CHAPTER 10

All around me people were screaming and running. Some were filming with their phones. I wanted to yell for them to stop, that those were my friends in there and they could be hurt, that it was partially my fault!

Was I too late?

"Suit-Lady! What happened? Are they okay?" I was desperate for any information.

"Engaging sonar hyperthermal analysis," the

suit responded. It whirled quickly, and my mask's view changed to almost an X-ray vision of the inside of the monument. *Waaaaaay* up at the top, I could see the elevator. A red circle appeared around it. That's where Ned, Liz, and the others were. "All elevator occupants appear to be alive."

"Oh thank God." I exhaled slightly.

Then she continued: "For the next eight minutes and twenty seconds."

"What?!"

"The elevator's structural integrity has been compromised, and it will fall."

My mind was scrambling for a plan when a familiar voice shouted what I should've been thinking. "What are you doing?! Help them!" Michelle was still standing, wide-eyed, next to me.

"Yeah, yeah, on it!" I said, not even bothering to use my Super Hero voice. There was no time—I had to get to the top of that monument!

Oh boy. The monument was huge. I could barely see the top. "How tall is this thing?" I wondered out loud.

"The Washington Monument is over five hundred and—"

"Not really helping!" I took one more look and leaped onto the monument. The highest I'd ever climbed was six stories. This was over five hundred feet.

And I needed to get to the top.

In eight minutes.

No problem.

(Gulp.)

From the hyperthermal analysis, it looked as if the elevator was about eight feet below the observation deck. Poor Ned and the others were probably so scared. Hopefully, they were close enough to the deck for park rangers to pry open the doors above them. They would have to be super careful—any sudden shift and the elevator could fall. It was only a matter of time either way. Were "alien bomb explosions" even covered in the training for the tour guides?

"The safety systems are completely failing," my suit informed me. Great. Could I catch a break and get some *good* news here? I kept climbing and climbing up the side of the monument. "The occupants are in imminent mortal danger. They will fall in seven minutes, twelve seconds."

"Not if I get there first," I said through gritted teeth. The top looked as far away as ever. I looked down to see how much progress I had made. Five stories, maybe? *Time to dig deep, Parker.* I psyched myself up, quickening my pace.

Please let them get Ned and Liz out safely, I thought. Who was I kidding? Flash would probably push to the front of the line. Whatever he did, he better not put my friends in greater danger.

"You now have two minutes, fifteen seconds," the suit updated me.

"What?!" That meant the elevator could drop any second.

"The structural deterioration has escalated."

Looking around, I was at a loss. All I could see was gray wall above and below me. "Whoa..." I groaned. Don't worry about below. "I gotta get in there! How can we do that? *Fast!*"

I heard a *CLICK* and a buzzing sound as the spider-symbol on my suit suddenly fell off... and started flying around me on its own!

"Deploying reconnaissance drone. Searching for entry point." My eyes started following the drone, amazed that it had been on me the whole time.

"Eight observation windows have been located," the suit said.

"Great! Point me in the right direction, and let's go!" I said, starting to move toward the nearest window.

"There are three occupants remaining in the elevator." *Hmm*, seems I was probably right about Flash. Three was a good number. I could handle three.

I reached the window of the observation deck and kicked at it. Nothing. "C'mon!"

"One minute, fifteen seconds," the suit updated.

I was just about to give the window another kick when—"Yipes!"

A flock of birds flew past my face out of nowhere, and I found myself in a free fall off the ledge. Instinct kicked in, and I fired a web at the edge of the window. I slammed into the side of monument.

"Thirty seconds."

Go time.

I climbed back up and was just about to try to punch through the window when I heard a *WHIP WHIP WHIP* behind me and the wind picked up. Turning, I saw a police helicopter. Help! At last!

Uh-oh. Maybe I spoke too soon. The police had snipers aiming my way! Did these guys not realize I was trying to *rescue* my friends? *"Return to the ground immediately,"* a voice rang out from a megaphone. Guess not.

"I'm trying to help them! They're about to die!" I yelled back, hoping they could hear me above the sound of the wind and whirling blades.

"Return or we will open fire!" That answered that.

Looking up, I realized I could see the top of the monument. If I could get there...

"Fifteen seconds."

I had run out of time to think. I made a break

141

for it, climbing as fast as possible. The helicopter angled slightly to increase altitude and follow me. Now the blades were positioned between me and the snipers. Sweet! Working so far.

I reached the tip-top and stood up, the helicopter almost even with me. Any moment and the snipers would be level with me again. Time to engage Plan Insanity.

"Five seconds."

No turning back. I took a deep breath and dove off the monument.

I flew straight at the helicopter, arcing over it.

THWIP! I fired my webs at the helicopter landing skid. It caught. Tucking into a roll, I swung back around. The window of the observation deck was rushing toward me.

"Zero seconds. The elevator roof is no longer attached."

The update came just as I crashed through the

window. I didn't even notice the other students on the landing. All I could hear were Ned and Liz screaming as the elevator started to drop.

TWHIP! BONK! BONK! FWIP! The ricochet web I fired down the elevator shaft found its mark, catching the elevator and stopping its fall. Then I fired another web and started to pull up the elevator, bracing my feet against the doorframe. I could see Ned and Liz and Mr. Harrington looking up at me, terrified—except Ned, who was giving me a thumbs-up.

I was doing it! It was working, I thought as I strained to haul three humans and an elevator up two stories. But then the elevator doors flew off and a gust of wind sucked me right into the shaft until—*WHAM!* I was on my back in the elevator, looking up at the three people I was trying to save.

"Hey," Ned said, smiling.

I gave a weak wave. "Hey."

Without any warning, the web I had anchored to the roof of the elevator gave out, and we started to fall again. Aiming at the top of the shaft, I fired another web, this time at the gears of the elevator. We slammed to a halt.

Adrenaline kicked in and I leaped up, bracing my feet against the remains of the roof. With all my might, I started to pull us up, up...higher... almost...there.

Finally, we'd gotten back to eye level with the other students on the landing. Mr. Harrington climbed out onto the observation deck and joined the others. Ned was right behind him.

"I knew you'd make it," he whispered as he climbed past me.

"That makes one of us," I muttered back.

I still needed to get Liz out, but she seemed paralyzed, too afraid to move. The roof started to groan, and I felt it give under my feet as I reached toward her.

"Take my hand!" I yelled to her.

Too late. The roof snapped off and the elevator began a free fall to the bottom, five hundred feet below.

"No!" I yelled again, finally jolting Liz out of her trance.

She reached out and almost reached my hand, but gravity won out and she started falling faster.

Bracing my feet for stability, I immediately shot a strand of webbing toward Liz's hands. *Yes!* The web caught and she hovered in midair as the elevator dropped down under her.

Seconds later a loud *BOOM* rang up through the shaft. The elevator had smashed into the ground. Liz, still connected to me by web, met my look. I wished I could tell her, *At least I wasn't late this time.* But I couldn't. The most important thing was, she was safe. I pulled us back up to the observation deck.

I swung her to the platform, and for a moment, it seemed as if it were just the two of us up there.

"You okay?" I asked. She seemed to have lost language and could only nod. I took that as a positive sign. "Good."

Looking around, everyone was staring at me in shock (except Ned, who was fist-pumping and grinning from ear to ear). Unsure of what to do, I stammered out, "I guess I should...I'm gonna go...now."

I shot a web at the ceiling and gave a slight, awkward wave as I slowly descended into the elevator shaft. As I got farther down, the faces of my friends looking down at me started to fade in the darkness.

Tony Stark's words echoed in my head: *Keep doing what you're doing, saving the little*

people... Except these weren't just "the little people"—they were my friends. As long as they were safe, everything would be okay.

I didn't need to wait for that call to be an Avenger. I was already Spider-Man.